The Let's Talk Library™

Let's Talk About Scratches, Scrapes, and Bug Bites

Melanie Apel Gordon

The Rosen Publishing Group's
PowerKids Press™
New York

For my "little" Gutmann Girls—Valerie, Laurie, and Michelle. With love, from your "big" babysitter!

Published in 2000 by The Rosen Publishing Group, Inc.
29 East 21st Street, New York, NY 10010

Copyright © 2000 by The Rosen Publishing Group, Inc.

First Edition

Book Design: Erin McKenna

Photo Illustrations by Debra Marcus Brown.

Gordon, Melanie Apel.
    Let's talk about scratches, scrapes, and bug bites / by Melanie Apel Gordon.
        p.   cm.— (The let's talk library)
    Includes index.
    Summary: Discusses how to care for various types of scratches, scrapes, and bug bites to prevent them from becoming infected.
    ISBN 0-8239-5416-1
    1. Wounds and injuries—Juvenile literature. 2 Bites and stings—Juvenile literature. 3. Wound healing—Juvenile literature. [1. Wounds and injuries. 2. Bites and stings. 3. Wound healing. 4. First aid.]
    I. Title. II. Series.
    RD93.G67 1998
    617.1—dc21   98-39849
                                                                                              CIP
                                                                                              AC

Manufactured in the United States of America

Contents

Busy Day

James and Ryan have been playing outdoors all day. Ryan climbed a tree. James in-line skated. He and Ryan rode their bicycles for a while. By the end of the day, James and Ryan had gotten pretty banged up. James scraped his knee. Ryan got a few scratches on his arm and a few more on his legs when he came down from the tree. Then James cried, "Ouch! I just got bitten by a bug!"

◀ Playing outdoors is lots of fun.
Always try to be safe.

Scratches and Scrapes

Everyone gets scratches and scrapes. When you fall down or brush up against something rough, you may scrape your skin. When you scratch or scrape yourself, you are **injuring** your skin. Sometimes you may bleed. Small scratches and scrapes usually bleed only for a little while. They usually take a few days to heal. And once they do, you may not even be able to tell where you had the scrape. Bigger and deeper scratches and scrapes may bleed longer and hurt a lot. When this happens, you need first aid.

Ask a grown-up to look at ▶
a scratch or a scrape.

First Aid

If your **wound** is bleeding a lot, press on it with a piece of cloth. This may hurt, but pressing on it will help stop the bleeding. You or a friend should try to find a grown-up who can help right away. Keep the wound covered until you can clean it. Cleaning with soap and water may sting, but it's very important. Soap will kill any **germs** that may have gotten into the cut. If you are really bleeding a lot, or if your wound hurts very much, tell a grown-up. You may have to go see the doctor.

◀ Always take care of a cut or scrape as soon as it happens.

Caring for a Wound

After you've cleaned your cut or scrape, cover it with a clean, dry bandage. A grown-up might put some **antibacterial ointment** on your wound. This will help it heal. Until the cut or scrape has healed, it's a good idea to keep it clean and covered. Change the bandage every day until a scab forms. Then, as long as it doesn't hurt, you can take the bandage off. Don't pick at the scab. That will just make it take longer for your scratch or scrape to heal.

As long as you keep your wound covered, you can do everything you normally do. ▶

Bug Bites

Another thing you have to look out for when you play outdoors is bugs. Bug bites can really bother you. Bug bites sometimes hurt. Often they itch. They may also swell or turn red. Even if your bug bites really itch, try not to scratch! You could make the bite bleed or it could get **infected** from any dirt on your fingers. If the bite gets infected, it will take longer for it to stop itching and heal.

◀ *Even though you want to scratch an itchy bug bite, try not to.*

Spray the Bugs Away

The best way to keep from getting bitten by a bug is to use an insect **repellant**. Insect repellants are **chemicals** that keep bugs away. There are different kinds of insect repellants. Bug sprays and **citronella** candles are the most common. Citronella is a chemical that bugs don't like. Be careful when you spray bug spray. Never spray it near someone's face. If you use a citronella candle, have a grown-up light it. And always be careful around lit candles.

Ask a grown-up to spray bug spray on you. ▶

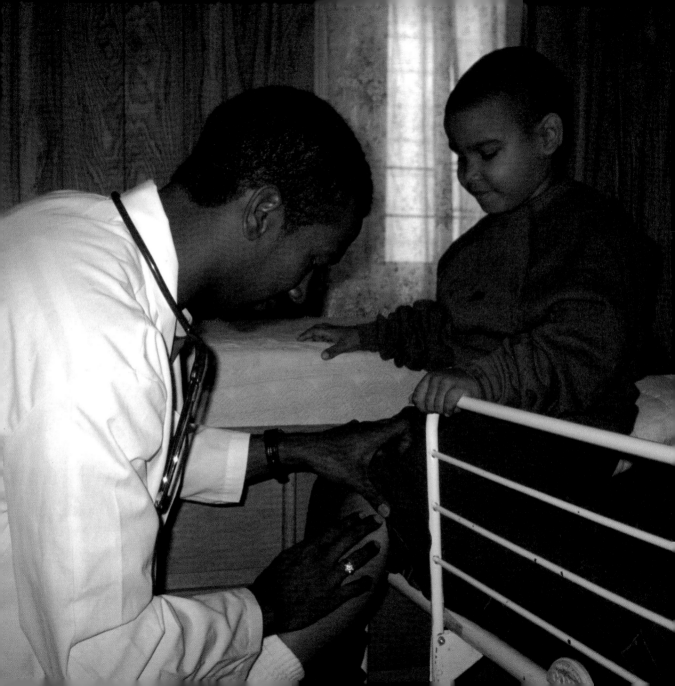

Doctor! Doctor!

You won't need to see a doctor for most bug bites. But if you start to feel sick after you've been bitten by a bug, you may be **allergic** to the bug bite. You may throw up or have a fever. It may be hard for you to breathe. Part of your body around the bug bite may swell up. If any of these things happen, tell a grown-up right away. You may have to go to the doctor.

◀ *A doctor can give you medicine for a bug bite if you need it.*

Itchy! Scratchy!

Bug bites often itch. Try hard to keep your fingers away. You can put ice on the bug bite to help stop the itching. Your mom or dad may put some **calamine** lotion on the bite. When you really want to scratch, try covering the bite with a cool washcloth or even some mud. But whatever you do, don't scratch!

Putting ice on the bug bite will make it numb, so you don't feel the itchiness anymore. ▶

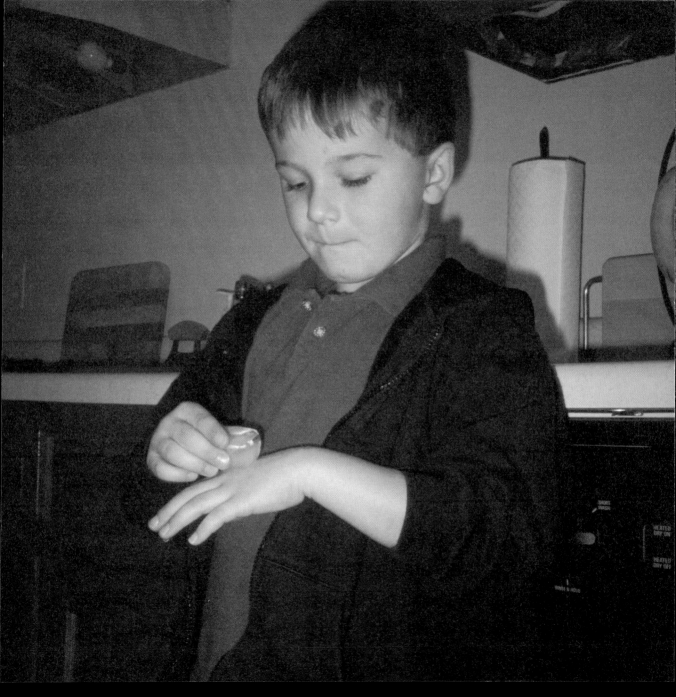

Things to Remember About Scratches and Scrapes

Taking care of your scratch or scrape will help it heal faster. These are things to remember when you get a scratch or scrape:

- Don't touch it with dirty hands.
- Wash it gently with soap and water.
- Cover it with a bandage.
- Don't scratch it, even if it itches.
- Don't pick at the scab.
- Use a new bandage every day.

Doing all of these things will help your skin heal nicely.

◀ *One of the most important things to remember about scratches and scrapes is to keep them clean.*

Bug Tips

Bug bites can be a real pain. The best thing to do with bug bites is to **avoid** them. If you know you'll be going where there are bugs, don't wear lotion that has a **fragrance**. Wear long sleeves and pants so the bugs can't get to your skin. Use an insect repellant spray or candle.

No matter whether you have a scratch, a scrape, or a bug bite, there are things you should always remember. Keep it clean, don't scratch, and if it hurts a lot or you feel sick, tell a grown-up.

Glossary

allergic (uh-LER-jik) Having a bad reaction to something.

antibacterial ointment (AN-ty-bak-TEER-ee-ul OYNT-mint) A greasy cream used to fight bacteria and germs on the skin.

avoid (uh-VOYD) To keep away from.

calamine (KA-luh-myn) A lotion that helps stop bites and rashes from itching.

chemical (KEH-mih-kul) A substance used to cause a reaction.

citronella (sih-truh-NEH-luh) Oil used in insect repellant candles.

fragrance (FRAY-grants) A sweet or nice smell.

germ (jerm) Something that can cause an infection.

infect (in-FEKT) To cause illness.

injure (IN-jer) To harm or damage.

repellant (rih-PEH-lunt) Something that makes other things, such as bugs, stay away.

wound (WOOND) An injury to the skin.

Index

ML